# How to Heal a Broken Wing

# How to Heal a Bro

ken Wing

BOB GRAHAM

WALKER BOOKS
AND SUBSIDIARIES
LONDON · BOSTON · SYDNEY · AUCKLAND

High above the city,

no one heard a soft thud of feathers against glass.

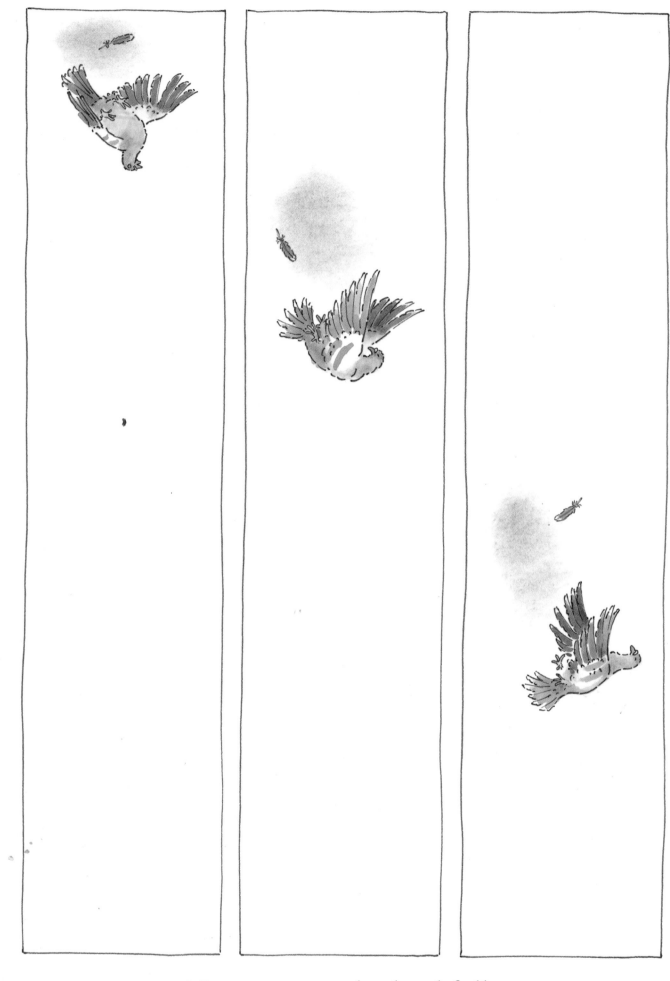

No one saw the bird fall.

No one looked.

Except Will.

Will saw a bird with a broken wing ...

and he took it home.

A loose feather can't be put back ...

but a broken wing can sometimes heal.

With rest …

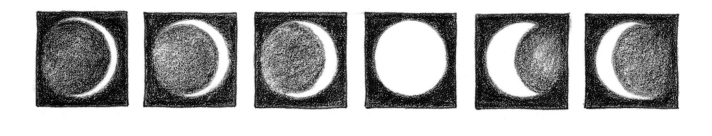

and time ...

and a little hope ...

a bird may fly again.

Will opened his hands …

and with a beat of its wings,
the bird was gone.

For Lyndsay and Ella

*With thanks to Rosie for her fabulous title lettering*

First published 2008 by Walker Books Ltd
87 Vauxhall Walk, London SE11 5HJ

2 4 6 8 10 9 7 5 3 1

© 2008 Blackbird Design Pty Ltd

The right of Bob Graham to be identified as author-illustrator of this work has been asserted by him in accordance with the Copyright, Designs and Patents Act 1988

This book has been typeset in Stempel Schneidler Light.

Printed in Singapore

British Cataloguing in Publication Data:
a catalogue record for this book is available from the British Library

ISBN 978-1-4063-0716-0

www.walkerbooks.com